Clifford THE BIG RED DOG®
Happy St. Patrick's Day, Clifford

by Quinlan B. Lee
Illustrated by Steve Haefele

Based on the Scholastic book series
"Clifford The Big Red Dog"
by Norman Bridwell

ISBN 978-0-545-23401-6

Designed by Michael Massen

12   11   10   9   15 16 17 18 19/0

Printed in the U.S.A.

First printing, February 2010   40

SCHOLASTIC INC.

New York   Toronto   London   Auckland
Sydney   Mexico City   New Delhi   Hong Kong

It was St. Patrick's Day.

Emily Elizabeth and Clifford were on their way to the big parade.

"You're my favorite Big Red Dog,"
said Emily Elizabeth. "But you need
something green. It will bring you luck!"

It was a chilly and very windy day.

Suddenly, a big gust blew by.

When Emily Elizabeth and Clifford got to
the parade, there were people everywhere.

There were fancy floats, Irish dancers,
and people playing bagpipes and fiddles.

Everything and everyone was green,
green, green!

Suddenly, Clifford felt someone pinch him.

"Ouch!"

"Sorry, big guy," said Cleo. "I had to do it.
You're not wearing any green."

"But I was wearing a leprechaun hat," said
Clifford. "I wonder what happened to it."

"Maybe a leprechaun stole it for himself."
T-Bone laughed. "They can be sneaky."

"Clifford," Emily Elizabeth called.

"Come on. The parade is about to begin."

Just then the wind blew again.

It tickled Clifford's nose.

Aaa . . . aaa . . . aaa . . . ACHOOOOO!

"Sorry," Emily Elizabeth told the marchers.

Clifford felt terrible.

He moved back . . . back . . . back . . .

. . . under the banner . . .

"Bad luck, buddy," T-Bone said.

"That's it!" called Cleo. "Quick!

Find something green."

The three dogs looked around.

"Clover!" said T-Bone. "Maybe we can find a four-leaf one."

Cleo wagged her tail. "That's lucky *and* green."

"I don't think that clover is a very good idea," said Clifford. "I think I'm aaa . . . aaa . . . AAAA . . . LLERGIC!!"

Clifford sneezed again.

Clifford hung his big red head.

"I've had enough bad luck for one day," he said. "I better go home."

"Clifford," called Emily Elizabeth. "The St. Patrick's Day float broke down, and we need your help."

Clifford stopped.

He wanted to help, but what if something else went wrong?

"Oh, I almost forgot! Look what Jetta found."
Emily Elizabeth handed Clifford his
leprechaun hat. "You'll look great wearing it in
the parade."

Something green!

Clifford ran to the float to help.

"Good luck!" his friends called.

Happy
St. Patrick's Day

Clifford led the parade down Main Street.
Behind him were the marchers and
flags, dancers doing their jig, bagpipes,
and fiddlers!

It was great!

But then another BIG gust of wind blew down the street.

Off went Clifford's green hat!

Clifford stopped and looked around.

He couldn't see the hat anywhere.

All he could see were his friends — Cleo,
T-Bone, Charley, Jetta, Sheriff Lewis, the
Bleekmans, Dr. Dihn.

And of course Emily Elizabeth.

They were all smiling and waving.

"You're doing great," called Emily Elizabeth.

"Looking good, big guy," Cleo barked.

Clifford wagged his tail.

He had great friends!

He might be big and red, without a bit of green, but he was still the luckiest dog around!

Do You Remember?

Circle the right answer.

1. What was Clifford allergic to?
   - a. His food
   - b. Balloons
   - c. Clover

2. Who found Clifford's hat?
   - a. T-Bone
   - b. Jetta
   - c. Charley

Which happened first?

Which happened next?

Which happened last?

Write a 1, 2, or 3 in the space after each sentence.

Clifford leads the St. Patrick's Day parade. _____

Clifford backs into the parade dancers. _____

Cleo pinches Clifford. _____